# Squid lifts the lid

Lesley Sims

Illustrated by David Semple

Behold the king's magician.
Her name is Splendid Squid.

Everybody loves her tricks
except for Sneaky Sid.

# Today Squid has a new trick.

She lifts the lid. The crown has gone!

Squid grins and puts the lid back down.

She lifts it up...

Splendid Squid

OH NO!

Squid sees Sid grin.

"I'll search each room and chest,"
Squid says. "And under every chair."

# Squid searches in the kitchen...

## ...and in the dining hall.

It isn't in the reading room...

...or where they hold a ball.

At last she tries a bathroom.
She lifts the toilet lid.

Sid creeps up from behind and shoves.

"Goodbye now! So long, Squid!"

Squid's flushed away!

She whooshes down.

...and lifts
another lid!

Squid squeezes out and looks about.
She spies a massive chest.

She lifts the lid and looks inside.

Sid's box of tricks

"The crown! Who would have guessed?"

Then Sid appears.

Sid's box
of tricks

"I'm sorry, Squid.
I shouldn't have flushed you down."

"I'm jealous of your magic skills.
It's why I hid the crown."

Squid smiles.
"Your trick was really good.
No need to feel bad, Sid."

That night, the king smiles in delight.

# Squid AND Sid lift a lid!

Splendid Squid
and her assistant Sid

# Starting to read

Even before children start to recognize words, they can learn about the pleasures of reading. Encouraging a love of stories and a joy in language is the best place to start.

**About phonics**

When children learn to read in school, they are often taught to recognize words through phonics. This teaches them to identify the sounds of letters that are then put together to make words. An important first step is for children to hear rhymes, which help them to listen out for the sounds in words.

You can find out more about phonics on the Usborne website at **usborne.com/Phonics**

**Phonics Readers**

These rhyming books provide the perfect combination of fun and phonics. They are lively and entertaining with great storylines and quirky illustrations. They have the added bonus of focusing on certain sounds so in this story your child will soon identify the *i* sound, as in **Squid** and **lid.** Look out, too, for rhymes such as **where** – **chair** and **hall** – **ball.**

**Reading with your child**

If your child is reading a story to you, don't rush to correct mistakes, but be ready to prompt or guide if needed. Above all, give plenty of praise and encouragement.

Edited by Jenny Tyler
Designed by Sam Whibley

Reading consultants: Alison Kelly and Anne Washtell

First published in 2024 by Usborne Publishing Limited, 83-85 Saffron Hill, London EC1N 8RT, United Kingdom.
usborne.com Copyright © 2024 Usborne Publishing Limited. The name Usborne and the Balloon logo are registered trade marks
of Usborne Publishing Limited.
UKE.